Daisy's Big Night

Daisy's
Big Night

Written by Sandra V. Feder

Illustrated by Susan Mitchell

Kids Can Press

For my mother, Shirley, who was creative, inspiring and loving — S.V.F.

For Lisa, my other sister — S.M.

Contents

Chapter One

Daisy liked running barefoot and feeling the blades of grass between her toes. She liked painting pictures and mixing colors to get the perfect shade of blue for the sky or pink for her best friend Emma's favorite shoes.

Daisy liked going to the mailbox to get the day's mail. She especially liked getting letters addressed to her, because they were full of interesting words that were meant for her eyes only. And more than painting or running barefoot, Daisy loved words. She collected her favorite words in a green notebook covered with purple polka dots.

Today, when she got the mail, Daisy was delighted to find a pretty pink envelope with her name on it. She thought it might be a party invitation from one of her friends, so she tried to think of someone who had a birthday in June. School would be ending soon and it would be a great time for a party, but Daisy couldn't think of anyone. Emma's birthday was in January and Samantha's was in October.

The envelope was quite big, though. It looked more like the sort of thing her mother received, inviting her to a baby shower or a dinner party. Daisy looked again to be sure she hadn't made a mistake. She was right! The envelope did have her name on it. With a loud "Yippee!" she ran inside.

The envelope was so pretty — pale pink with a trail of little blue flowers along the bottom edge — that Daisy hated to rip it open. On the other hand, she couldn't wait to find out what was inside. So she got the letter opener from her father's desk, carefully slit just the very top and pulled out the card. She was surprised by what she saw.

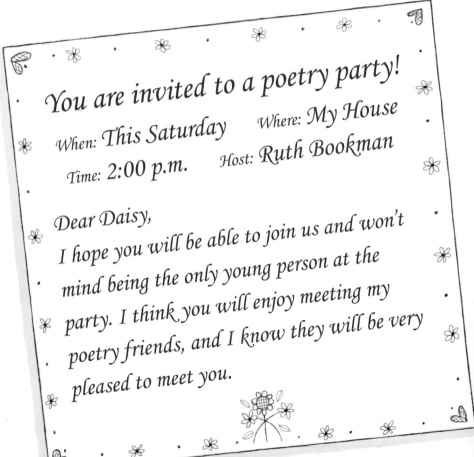

You are invited to a poetry party!

When: This Saturday   Where: My House
Time: 2:00 p.m.   Host: Ruth Bookman

Dear Daisy,

I hope you will be able to join us and won't mind being the only young person at the party. I think you will enjoy meeting my poetry friends, and I know they will be very pleased to meet you.

Daisy was thrilled! She hurried to the kitchen to tell her mom.

"Mrs. Bookman invited me to a poetry party!" she exclaimed. "It's a grown-up party, Saturday at two. Please, may I go?"

"That's quite an honor," said Daisy's mother, looking at the invitation. "I think you'll really have fun hearing all kinds of poems." She went to check the family calendar. "It looks clear to me," she said.

Daisy wanted to respond right away. Mrs. Bookman lived nearby, and Daisy thought about biking over to her house. But then she decided it would be faster to call, so she rushed to the phone instead. Mrs. Bookman didn't answer, so Daisy left a message. "Hi! It's Daisy. I'd love to come to the poetry party. Thanks so much for inviting me!"

Then she took the beautiful invitation and tacked it up on the bulletin board in her room for safekeeping.

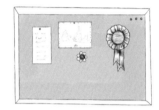

* * *

From then on, the poetry party was all Daisy could think about. At dinner, she told her father and her younger sister, Lily, about the invitation. "I'm so excited!" Daisy said. "I get to go to a party with real poets."

She thought for a minute. "I wonder what I should wear. Do you think a poetry party is like a garden party?" she asked. "I've seen pictures of those in books." She imagined herself in a flowing summer dress, a large floppy hat and white gloves.

"The party sounds very interesting," her father said. "But I don't think I will be much help picking an outfit."

Daisy was still thinking about the poetry party as she lay in bed that night. She wondered if she should bring a poem. Then she sat straight up, her brow furrowed. "Do all poems have to rhyme?" she whispered. She thought about the poems she and her friends wrote at school. Most of those did rhyme, but making everything rhyme was hard work.

Daisy turned on her bedside lamp and reached for her green notebook with the purple polka dots. She flipped to her list of

Favorite Rhyming Words. She read the words *sweet* and *treat* as well as *sun* and *fun*. Those would all be good words to work into a poem. But she wasn't exactly sure how to put the words together.

Daisy lay down again. She was feeling confused. Rhyming words like *flower* and *power*, poems she had heard before and Mrs. Bookman's invitation all bounced around in her head. When Daisy finally fell asleep, she dreamed that it was Saturday afternoon and she was arriving at Mrs. Bookman's house for the poetry party. When Mrs. Bookman opened the door, she spoke in rhyme.

Welcome, my dear,

So glad to have you here!

Would you like a treat?

Perhaps something sweet?

Please come and sit.

We'll begin in a bit!

In her dream, Daisy the poet thought of many wonderful responses.

Thanks a bunch,

I'd love a munch!

I can't wait.

This is great!

But when she opened her mouth, all that came out was a simple "Thank you," as she grabbed a treat. The other poets were gathered in the living room, and they were all speaking in rhyme, too. One of the women wore large glasses and a beautiful shawl. Another had a flower tucked behind one ear and her hair

piled on top of her head. And one of the men
had on a vest and a bow tie. In her dream,
Daisy sat down, feeling rather small as the
poets wove their words into lovely poems
around her.

Chapter Two

The next morning, Daisy couldn't wait to tell Emma about the poetry party. She rushed through breakfast and was waiting when Emma came down the street.

"Mrs. Bookman invited me to a poetry party on Saturday," Daisy said as they headed to school. "I'm excited but really nervous. I even made up a new word — *poetrified*. It means being petrified about poetry."

"That should definitely go on your *Made-Up Words* list," Emma said. "But why are you so scared?" Daisy told Emma the strange dream about the rhyming Mrs. Bookman.

"I don't think you have to worry," Emma said. "My mom is in Mrs. Bookman's poetry group, and she writes lots of different kinds of poems. Her favorites are haiku poems. They don't rhyme at all."

"Really?" Daisy asked.

"Yes," Emma assured her. "You count the syllables in each line of the poem, but you don't have to make them rhyme."

"I don't know how to count syllables either!

Maybe I just shouldn't go," Daisy said.

"You should go," Emma encouraged her. "My mom says that counting syllables is like counting beats — just — like — this." Emma demonstrated by tapping out three beats for the words *just, like, this,* against her leg. "Anyway, Mrs. Bookman wouldn't have invited you unless she thought you'd like it."

Daisy was quiet for a minute. She supposed Emma was right. Mrs. Bookman knew Daisy and wouldn't expect her to be a poetry expert. Daisy sighed.

"Okay, I'll go," she said. "But what should I wear?"

"My mom wears regular clothes when she meets with the poetry group," Emma said.

"But this isn't just a regular meeting. It's a party," Daisy pointed out. "I think I should look a little special."

"How about your new beret and your sparkly flower necklace?" Emma suggested.

"*Coolio!*" Daisy said. It was one of the words she and Emma had made up together, and it meant that something was really great. Daisy was relieved to have a plan, and she started to look forward to the party again.

When the girls arrived at school, their teacher could barely wait for her students to take their seats. "I have an idea!" Miss Goldner announced.

Daisy and Emma looked at each other with excitement. Miss Goldner's ideas were always great. That's because she was the best teacher ever and liked having fun almost as much as her students did. Daisy especially loved Miss Goldner's dance breaks. She seemed to know when her students couldn't sit still and concentrate on schoolwork anymore. She'd stop whatever it was they were doing and announce that it was time for a dance break. Music would fill the room as the students and Miss Goldner spun and twirled. Daisy wondered if Miss Goldner would suggest a daylong dance break or a students-versus-teachers dance contest.

"As all of you know, I'm getting married this summer and moving away. I won't be teaching here next year." Miss Goldner's eyes got a little misty. "So I wanted to come up with something really special we could do to celebrate how great this year has been. Instead of the usual Open House night for the end of the school year, let's have a Student Showcase! I will still put out your artwork and completed assignments, so your families can see what we've done this year. But I also want them to see all your special talents! For example, Roberto might want to demonstrate how to solve math problems."

All the students nodded in agreement, because Roberto really was terrific at math.

"But it doesn't have to be only school subjects that we showcase," Miss Goldner continued. "I want parents to know about the things you do outside of school, too. Emma can do ballet, if she would like."

"Yes!" Emma said quickly, confirming that she would like that very much.

Miss Goldner put up a large, glittery poster she had made to announce the showcase. "We'll have such a big night!" she exclaimed, as she put in the last tack.

Then it was time for spelling, but with all the excitement, even Daisy had a hard time keeping her mind focused on words.

At recess, all the kids were talking about the showcase. "I'm going to have a geography corner with a map of the world," Kevin said. "I'll ask people to point to a country, any one they want, and I'll tell them the capital city."

The other students knew this was something Kevin really liked and was very good at doing.

"Maybe I can show everyone my handball serve," Samantha said. Daisy and Emma liked that idea. Samantha did have a powerful serve.

"What will you do, Daisy?" Samantha asked.

Daisy had been thinking about the big night, but she didn't have any ideas yet. "I'll think of something," she said. She hoped she sounded more confident than she felt.

Chapter Three

The next day was Saturday, and Daisy woke
up still wondering what she should do for the
showcase. But she decided she'd better put it
out of her mind, so she could concentrate on
getting ready for the poetry party.

With her mother's help, she was making
her special, large, circle cookies to take to
Mrs. Bookman's house. When they were out of
the oven and cooling, Daisy sat for a minute,
trying to decide how to decorate them. She

would use at least three different colors of frosting, of course, but what design should she make?

The whole reason she loved making such big, round cookies was that there were so many ways to decorate them. One time, she had made them look like ladybugs, and another time, like flying saucers. As she sat thinking, she noticed her notebook open to her list of *Favorite Rhyming Words*. "That's it!" she said.

She started by making some white frosting. When it was done, she divided it into three bowls. Then she worked hard making blue frosting. She added one drop of food coloring

at a time and stirred
carefully until the color
exactly matched the
little blue flowers on the
invitation. Next,
she added coloring
to the other bowls until

she had beautiful shades of yellow and pink.

She put seven cookies out on the counter,

because there would be six people at the

party, and she thought it would be good to

have one extra.

Daisy used a knife to cover half of each

cookie with yellow frosting and half with

pink. Then she put the blue frosting into a pastry bag. Daisy looked at her notebook and carefully piped the word *sun* onto the yellow part of one cookie. Keeping her hands as steady as possible, she wrote the word *fun* on the pink part of the same cookie. The next cookie got the words *sweet* and *treat.* Then Daisy wrote more of her favorite rhyming words on the cookie tops. *Flower* and *power, bright* and *light, look* and *book.* She didn't want to repeat any words, so she added two new pairs to her list and then to her cookies — *ring* and *sing,* then *yellow* and *mellow.*

Attracted by the smell of the cookies and the promise of some frosting, Lily came bounding into the kitchen.

"These are pretty!" Lily said. "What do they say?"

Daisy read Lily the rhyming words. When she got to the cookie with the words *flower* and *power* on it, she noticed that she had smudged some of the letters.

"This one says, 'Please eat me!'" Daisy said playfully. She broke the cookie in two and handed half to Lily. Her dad, who had just wandered in, got the other half. After dabbing a bit more frosting on her piece, Lily happily popped it into her mouth.

"Yummy!" she declared.

"I couldn't have said it better myself," Dad agreed. "Any others that you want us to take off your hands?"

"Thanks, anyway," Daisy said, shooing

them away. She carefully decorated another cookie. When she was done, she cleaned up the kitchen and ate a quick lunch. Then it was time to get ready for the party.

First Daisy tried on her polka-dot dress and silver flats. Too fancy, she decided. Next she tried an all-black outfit — a flouncy skirt, long-sleeved black T-shirt and black tights. Too dark, she thought. Finally, she put on her favorite dress, a simple yellow one with a zipper up the front. She added her new purple beret and her favorite sparkly flower necklace. "Poetry perfect!" she declared to her image in the mirror.

Lily helped Daisy place her word cookies on

a large platter. Daisy was at the front door with the platter in her hands when Lily called out, "Don't forget your notebook!"

"I don't think I'll need it," Daisy said.

"But you take it everywhere," Lily reminded her.

Before Daisy could reply, Lily picked up the notebook and tucked it under Daisy's arm.

"There," Lily said. "Now you're ready."

Daisy giggled and headed out the door.

Chapter Four

Even though Lily had made her giggle and Emma had been reassuring, Daisy was still *poetrified.* As she walked up to Mrs. Bookman's door, she became even more nervous. How was she going to ring the doorbell with her hands full of cookies and her notebook wedged under her arm? She thought for a minute and then used her elbow.

"Daisy! Let me help you with that,"

Mrs. Bookman said as she took the platter and ushered Daisy into the kitchen.

"This is Daisy," Mrs. Bookman said, setting the platter down and making introductions. "Daisy, this is Shirley and this is Joan."

Daisy noticed Shirley's big smile and short, curly hair.

"I love your necklace," Shirley said.

"Thank you. Your scarf is pretty," Daisy replied, pointing to the scarf looped around Shirley's neck.

Joan, who was the tallest person there, was helping to arrange the food. She gave Daisy a friendly wave.

"This is Sam," Mrs. Bookman said, pointing to the only man in the room. Even though Sam didn't look any older than Daisy's dad, Daisy noticed that his cap was like the one her grandfather used to wear. It had a small visor and was made out of tweedy fabric. It made him look a bit old-fashioned, Daisy thought.

"And you know Emma's mom," Mrs. Bookman continued. Daisy gave Emma's mom a little hug.

"Let's all get a treat before we sit down," Mrs. Bookman said.

Daisy suddenly remembered her dream. When she realized that Mrs. Bookman wasn't speaking in rhyme, Daisy let out a big sigh of relief and began to relax.

Everyone admired Daisy's word cookies. "How clever!" Shirley said.

"Daisy is very fond of words," Mrs. Bookman explained to her guests. Daisy relaxed a little more. When everyone had a treat and something to drink, they headed out to the patio.

"Who wants to start?" Mrs. Bookman asked. Daisy wasn't sure what was supposed to get started, so she decided she would just sit quietly and listen.

"I will," said Joan. "I've been working on this poem for such a long time, but I can't find the right word to end it. I have spent so many days thinking about this one word."

Daisy couldn't believe what she had heard! "You spent how long thinking about one word?" Daisy asked, forgetting her plan to keep quiet.

"Well, I guess about two weeks," Joan said. "That must sound silly to you. I want it to be just right and ..."

"That's fantastic!" Daisy blurted out.

Joan looked surprised but pleased.

"I thought I was the only one who

thought about every word so carefully," Daisy explained.

"Do you write a lot of poems?" Shirley asked.

"Not really," Daisy said, turning her notebook over in her hands. She wasn't quite sure what to say next.

Mrs. Bookman jumped in to help. "Daisy makes wonderful word lists," she said. "She collects all sorts of words that interest her. Maybe she'll share some with us later."

Daisy nodded, although she still felt a bit unsure. She turned her attention to Joan, who had started reading her poem. It was about a

bird nesting outside
her window. The
last line of the poem

was about the author settling in for sleep and
seeing the little bird doing the same.

"I whispered a soft good-night," Joan read.
Then she explained her concern. "Good-night
just seems too flat, too ordinary, but I can't
think of anything else."

"Good-bye?" Shirley suggested.

"Sweet dreams?" Mrs. Bookman tried.

"Do birds dream?" Emma's mother asked.

Daisy thought for a minute as the poets
continued their discussion. Then she opened

her notebook to her list of *Quiet-Time Words*. *Good-night* and *sweet dreams* were there, but Daisy agreed they weren't quite right. Then she saw it. The word she knew would work beautifully with the quiet tone and sound of the poem.

"*Hush-a-bye*," she offered.

Joan tried it out. "I whispered a soft *hush-a-bye*."

"That's lovely," Mrs. Bookman said, and the others agreed.

Daisy was proud that she had been able to help. Emma's mother was next with a haiku. She explained to Daisy that haiku poems have three lines. "The ones I write have five syllables in the first line, seven syllables in the second line and then five again in the last line. They are often about the seasons or about nature," she said. She read hers.

Light is filtered through
delicate leaves of tall trees.
Shadows glide around.

"I feel like I'm right there in the woods!" Mrs. Bookman said. The other poets made a few comments as well. Then Sam read an ode, which he explained was a poem praising something or someone. Daisy loved his "Ode to Elvis." At first she didn't understand why he was talking about floppy ears and warm fur instead of guitars and funny hair. But she soon realized that Elvis was the name of his childhood puppy.

Daisy liked Shirley's poem about collecting shells on the beach, and how every other line rhymed. Mrs. Bookman's poem was in free verse. "It doesn't have to follow a pattern like haiku, or have words that rhyme, like other types of poetry. But it can if you want," Mrs. Bookman told her. "In this one, I tried to paint a picture with words." She began to read.

Like an old friend

come to visit,

we don't miss a beat.

At first it didn't sound like poetry, but as Mrs. Bookman continued, the flow of words began to make a picture in Daisy's mind.

I open the cover

and letters glide,

a black and white waltz.

Thoughts and ideas

move and swirl,

and make my mind leap.

Happily I return,

again and again

to the dance of my book.

Daisy couldn't believe so few words could make her feel so much! She had always loved books but had never thought about a book as an old friend or about how the ideas and letters sometimes seemed to dance off the page. Now, she couldn't wait to get home and curl up with one of her favorites.

Mrs. Bookman suggested a break. When the poets came back with their snacks, Mrs. Bookman turned to Daisy. "Would you like to share one of your word lists?" she asked.

As much as Daisy loved her word lists, she felt a little shy about reading them out loud. But if anyone would appreciate them, it would be this group. So she took a deep breath and opened her notebook. Daisy read one of her favorites, her list of *Perfectly Paired Words*. She read, *"Bouncy balls, chunky chocolate, comfy couches, flying flags, summer sun."* The poets all said how much they liked the words she had put together.

Encouraged by their responses, Daisy said, "The haiku reminded me of nature, so I think I'll read my *Cloud Words* list now." She looked

into her notebook and read, *"Cotton candy,*
white, gray, floating, wispy, fluffy, puffy."

"Daisy, that list is practically a poem
already!" Shirley exclaimed.

Daisy beamed. She wanted to ask Shirley what she meant by the list being a poem already, but the poets had moved on to discussing a date for their next get-together. Then everyone started saying their good-byes, and Shirley left before Daisy could talk to her. Daisy helped Emma's mom and Mrs. Bookman clean up. The two women began discussing a new restaurant in town, and Daisy didn't want to interrupt to ask about Shirley's comment.

She picked up her notebook and her platter, which was now empty. As Mrs. Bookman walked Daisy to the door, she said, "I knew you would add so much to the party, and you did!"

"Thanks!" Daisy said. "I didn't know what it would be like, but I had a really good time."

As she headed home, she glanced at her notebook, which was tucked tightly under her arm. She had always guarded it carefully. But now, thinking her lists could be the seeds from which poems grew, it felt even more special.

Chapter Five

As she headed down the street, Daisy saw
Samantha and Tyler. Her two classmates were
deep in conversation.

"Hi," Daisy called, as she got closer.

"Daisy!" said Samantha. "We're talking
about the showcase. I've been practicing
my handball serve, and I even made a chart
showing different kinds of serves."

"That's great," Daisy said.

"What are you going to do?" Samantha

asked. Daisy still wasn't sure, but before she could answer, Tyler jumped in.

"You're good at finding words," he said, pointing to the notebook under Daisy's arm. "I'm good at spelling them. That's what I'm going to do at the showcase — spell. I won the school spelling bee," he said proudly.

Daisy had been impressed by his win. She loved finding special words, learning their meanings and using them in fun ways. But she didn't always pay attention, at first, to spelling. If she wasn't sure how one of her wonderful words was spelled, she looked it up in her dictionary before putting it into her notebook.

"Spelling sounds great for the showcase," Daisy said.

She turned and headed home, thinking again about what she was going to do for the big night.

***

At dinner, Daisy was still worried about the showcase, but she couldn't wait to tell her family about the poetry party. "I really liked Sam's 'Ode to Elvis,'" Daisy said. "He sure loved his dog."

"I'm not old, I'm young!" Lily announced, sticking her chin up in the air to make her point.

"I didn't say 'old,'" Daisy corrected, "I said 'ode.'"

"What's ode?" Lily asked.

Daisy explained that an ode was a kind of poem that praised something or someone.

"People write odes when they really care about something," Daisy's mother added.

"I could write one about you!" Daisy's dad said, making a deep bow toward his wife.

"Good idea," she said. "But you would have so much to say that it would go on for pages and pages!"

Everyone laughed.

Then it was time for Daisy to clear the dishes and for Lily to wipe the table. After playing a game with Lily, Daisy sat at her desk in front of her open notebook. Even though she was in her pajamas, she was still wearing her beret and sparkly

necklace. She wasn't ready for the wonderful day of poetry to end.

Using her dictionary to check the spellings, she made a new list called *Poetry Words*. She wrote *ode, haiku, rhyme* and *free verse*. She remembered Sam's "Ode to Elvis." She liked the old-fashioned words in his poem and how he seemed to be talking directly to the puppy. Daisy thought about things that meant a lot to her. Her eyes landed on her list of *Sweetest Words*. She added something new to the list and then got right to work.

Chapter Six

The next day was Sunday. After lunch, Daisy went to visit Mrs. Bookman. "I wrote an ode," she announced excitedly when Mrs. Bookman opened the door.

"Wonderful!" Mrs. Bookman exclaimed. "May I hear it?"

"My mom said an ode should show how much you care about something," Daisy said. She started reading quietly, her voice getting louder as she reached the end.

Ode to Ice Cream

Oh, ice cream, you make me so happy!

You are cold and sweet.

Fudge runs slowly down.

A cherry is your crown.

My spoon sinks deep.

My mouth waters.

Sweet sundae, you are all mine!

Mrs. Bookman clapped her hands in delight. "I love it!" she said. "And I think I know just what our snack should be today." Daisy and Mrs. Bookman each got a bowl from the cabinet. Mrs. Bookman went to the freezer, and they began scooping. Although Daisy usually liked the interesting snacks Mrs. Bookman offered, she was happy to have ice cream today.

"When did you start writing poetry?" Daisy asked.

"After I graduated from college,"
Mrs. Bookman said. "At that time, it seemed
as if there were poets everywhere. You could
walk down the street or into a café, and people
would be discussing words and sharing ideas.
It was magical! You would have loved it,
Daisy."

People sitting around talking about words!
"It does sound wonderful!" Daisy agreed,
trying to imagine what that must have felt like.

Daisy thanked Mrs. Bookman for the ice
cream and for telling her about the "golden
poetry days," as Mrs. Bookman liked to call
them. Then Daisy went to find Emma. All

week long, they had been planning to spend the afternoon playing by the creek. Now it was time, and Daisy couldn't wait. She loved spending time outdoors with Emma.

***

The shallow creek gurgled around their ankles as the best friends splashed each other. Daisy thought about the words *splish* and *splash*. They reminded her of words she had heard the poets use. She loved how closely the poets looked at the world, especially nature. Daisy tried to do the same. She reached over and picked a small wildflower that was just beginning to open. "It's growing,"

she said, showing it to Emma.
Then she imagined herself
in her poet's beret.

"It's blossoming," she tried.

"Very poetic!" Emma exclaimed.

The girls picked more wildflowers and then
sat beside the creek weaving them into chains.
They pretended to be princesses in their
wildflower crowns and walked with their heads
held high. After chasing each other through
the moat of their imaginary palace, they lay
down on the grass. "Let's count the trees in
our kingdom," Emma suggested.

"Don't you mean our *princessdom*?" Daisy

asked with a grin. She hopped up and grabbed
a large stick to use as a sword.

"We're modern princesses," Emma declared,
finding a sword of her own and swinging it
around. "We know how to defend ourselves!"

"We are so *coolio*!" Daisy agreed, hitting

Emma's sword with her own and yelling, "Touché!" They laughed as they ran from tree to tree defending their *princessdom* from invaders. Finally, it was time to lay down their swords. Muddy and happy, the girls headed home.

Daisy hadn't wanted to bring her notebook to the creek, but once she got cleaned up, she was eager to write down words about the afternoon. She put on her wildflower crown and began a *Nature Words* list. She wrote *green, gurgle, rocks, trees, splish* and *splash* on it. Finally, she added *wildflowers*.

***

After supper, Daisy had
fun playing a quiet game of
cards with her family. As her
dad shuffled the deck, Daisy

described the Student Showcase that
Miss Goldner was planning. It would take
place the evening before the last day of school.

"It's going to be a really big night," Daisy
told them.

"What will you do?" her mom asked.

"I don't know," Daisy said. "I guess I could
show how to do a soccer penalty kick or how to
paint a flower. I'm pretty good at those things."

"Yes, you are," her father agreed.

"But they don't seem special enough," Daisy said. "After all, it's one of my last times with Miss Goldner. On the final day of school, we only stay until noon. And the morning is so busy with the end-of-year assembly and taking things down from the walls that there won't be much time with her at all. That's why the showcase is so important. I have to think of something really special." Daisy wished she knew what her special thing should be.

Chapter Seven

The next day was science day, and because Miss Goldner always made science fun, Daisy and Emma arrived at school early. When they got to the classroom, they were amazed by what they saw. There were pieces of wire on one desk, little batteries and lightbulbs on another, and pipe cleaners on yet another. Scraps of fabric and cardboard littered the floor, and gears were scattered on a table.

Then they saw Miss Goldner. She was wearing a lab coat that had been tie-dyed in bright colors, and she had on large, funny glasses.

"Welcome to our laboratory," she said as the students came in. "All year long, we've learned about different aspects of science. Today, you get to put it all to use. We'll break up into groups, and you can invent something!"

The students eagerly grabbed supplies and got to work. Daisy's group decided to make a tool that would allow teachers to write and erase more easily at the top of the chalkboard. They had noticed that Miss Goldner couldn't reach the top without standing on a chair. So they made a Teacher's Helper — a long stick that had a place to attach a piece of chalk or a marker for a whiteboard, and an eraser. Miss Goldner tried it out right away.

"It's marvelous!" she declared, grinning. She wrote a reminder about the Student Showcase at the very top of the board. "Now everyone can see it, and it won't be erased by accident."

Emma's group decided to tackle the water bottle problem. Miss Goldner let her students keep water bottles on their desks, but every week at least one spilled and made a mess. Even when they didn't spill, the bottles took up precious space. So the students in Emma's group came up with an idea for a water bottle sling. It would hang on the back of a chair, freeing up desk space and cutting down on spills. For their invention, they used fabric, wire and rubber bands. It worked so well that soon everybody wanted one.

The day passed quickly for the inventors in Room 8. At the end of the day, Miss Goldner praised all the different inventions and promised to display them at the Student Showcase.

It had been such a good day and so much fun being an inventor! Daisy knew she wanted to remember it and all the other fun things they had done that year. "I'll just be a few minutes," she told Emma.

"I'll wait on the playground," Emma said, waving as she left the room.

Daisy sat quietly at her desk with her notebook open in front of her. She thought about the great inventions they had made that day. She remembered the wonderful words she had heard as the students admired each other's work. And she recalled other special moments from the school year. Suddenly she called out, "I've got it!" Miss Goldner turned around. "Oh, sorry," Daisy said. "I'm making a new word list."

"Great," Miss Goldner replied.

"Exactly!" Daisy said as she wrote the title of her new list: *Room 8 Words*. She included *giggles, inventing, sharing* and *dancing*. Then Daisy added *awesome, great* and *spectacular* to describe how she felt about all they had done. She was so pleased with her new list that she did a little happy dance. She knew this list would help her remember an *awesome* day and an amazing year.

On the way home, Emma told Daisy about the video her father was helping her make for the Student Showcase. In it, Emma would show how a pirouette was done. She was also planning to wear her leotard and ballet slippers at the showcase, so she could demonstrate all five ballet positions.

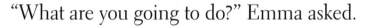

"That sounds super!" Daisy said.

"What are you going to do?" Emma asked.

"I still haven't decided," Daisy answered. "I do need to figure it out soon. I've only got two more days."

Daisy tried to smile, but she was getting worried. She hadn't come up with anything yet, and now time was running out.

Emma started up her driveway but spun around and ran back to where Daisy was standing. "You'll come up with something great," Emma reassured her with a hug. "After all, you're *Delightfully Different Daisy*!"

This time, Daisy really did smile. *Delightfully Different Daisy* was the special name she had given herself. She had tried many different words before deciding that *delightful* and *different* were the ones that she most liked to describe herself. Daisy had been determined to find the right name, and it must have worked because Emma remembered and used it. Now, Daisy was determined to find the right thing for the showcase.

***

With Emma's encouraging words in her head, Daisy spent the rest of the walk home thinking about all the things she did well. Jumping rope, making frosting and weaving wildflower chains all came to mind. But Daisy wasn't convinced any of those were right for the showcase.

When she got home, she looked in on Bubbles. Life seemed so simple for her pet fish. "You're really good at swimming," Daisy said, sprinkling a little fish food in the bowl and watching Bubbles gobble it up. Daisy went up to her room and looked around.

Her soccer ball was in the corner, and her painting supplies were on the shelf. But she had already ruled out those activities. Her eyes landed on her green notebook with the purple polka dots. She went over to her desk, opened the notebook and looked at some of her favorite word lists. She was really good at collecting words. Was there a way to turn her love of words into something wonderful for the showcase?

Daisy sat down and thought about it some more. Then she saw the invitation for the poetry party on her bulletin board. That made her think about Mrs. Bookman. Daisy picked up her notebook and turned it over in her hands.

Suddenly she knew exactly what she would do! Daisy grabbed her pen. She was concentrating so hard that her mother had to call her three times before

Daisy heard her and bounded down the stairs for dinner.

Daisy asked her mother if they could make cookies when they were done eating.

"Sure," her mother said. "Any special reason?"

"It's a surprise," said Daisy. "Lily, I'll need your help, too."

"At your service," Lily said, giving Daisy a happy salute.

Chapter Eight

The next day, the classroom didn't look quite as messy as it had on inventing day, but it wasn't exactly neat and tidy either. That's because students had started bringing in posters and props for the showcase the following night. There was a large map of the world that Kevin was using for his geography corner. Roberto had a new box of chalk for doing math problems on the board. Emma and her dad had finished the ballet video, and it was tucked in the dance bag under Emma's desk.

"Miss Goldner," Daisy asked, "will we be able to use our desks at the showcase?"

"Of course," Miss Goldner replied. "Do you need anything else, Daisy?" Most of the other students had some kind of supplies or props.

"I'll have everything I need by tomorrow night," Daisy said confidently.

* * *

After school, with Lily's help, Daisy loaded a large bag. She put in a small striped tablecloth, her beret and her sparkly flower necklace. Next, she decorated the cookies

with rhyming words, the way she had for
Mrs. Bookman's poetry party, and Lily
carefully placed them in a tin. Then Daisy
went to her room and took out her notebook.
She looked at her list of *Nature Words* and
decided to try writing a haiku.

She remembered that when she and Emma were at the creek, they had talked about all the different colors of green they saw around them. She tried many times before she got the correct number of syllables in each line and had a haiku that she really liked. Then she thought about Emma and how delighted she had been with some of the wildflowers they had seen. Daisy counted beats until she had a second haiku completed.

After dinner, Daisy couldn't wait to get back to her writing. She remembered Shirley's comment about how her *Cloud Words* list was almost a poem already. She never had asked Shirley or Mrs. Bookman what that meant.

"I guess I'll have to figure it out for myself," she said.

Daisy looked at the *Cloud Words* list. All the words described clouds. She remembered Joan's poem about the bird outside her window and how the poem was mostly a description of what she saw. "Maybe I can make a poem about watching clouds," Daisy said.

After she had covered several sheets of paper with writing, Daisy felt sure she had it just right. She entered the poem into her notebook along with the completed haiku

poems. Next, she took out some markers and
construction paper and made some props
for the showcase. Then she used a large
piece of poster board to make one more item.
When she was finished, she put everything
in her bag.

The last thing she needed to do was to make a phone call.

"Hi, Mrs. Bookman, it's Daisy," she said when Mrs. Bookman answered. "Can you come to my Student Showcase tomorrow night? I think you'll really like it."

"I'd love to come, Daisy," Mrs. Bookman said.

Daisy went to bed happy. That night she dreamed about poems dancing off the pages of her notebook in a slow waltz.

Chapter Nine

Although Miss Goldner tried to teach her students the next day, they were all so excited about the showcase that they couldn't concentrate. So Miss Goldner had them help her clean the classroom instead. Finally, it was time to set up, and the students sprang into action. They put up signs and posters and took out balls and videos. Daisy calmly pushed her desk into a corner at the back of the room. She took out the striped tablecloth and draped it over the desk. Next, she brought over a couple of extra chairs and arranged them around the desk. She put the cookies on a plate, quickly covering them so no one would eat them. Finally, she hung her sign on the wall behind her desk, turning it over so that no one could see what it said. She wanted it to be a surprise.

* * *

That night for dinner Daisy's mother made macaroni and cheese, which was Daisy's favorite. But Daisy was almost too excited to eat. Even Lily ate less than usual, and soon both girls asked to be excused to get ready for the showcase.

Daisy decided to wear black leggings and a long, swingy top. She let her curls go free. Lily put on her favorite striped dress and tights. When everyone was ready, Daisy's family walked the few blocks to school with Emma's family and Mrs. Bookman.

At the school, the girls went in ahead of the others to finish setting up. Daisy took her sparkly necklace and beret out of her bag and put them on. She placed the construction paper pages and her notebook on the desk. Finally, she turned her sign around and sat down.

Above her the sign proclaimed:

Welcome to Daisy's Word Café

Tyler was the first to spot Daisy's sign. He hurried over, looking worried.

"What's a Word Café?" he asked. "Do you spell words like I do?"

Welcome to
Daisy's Word Café

"No," Daisy said. "At my Word Café, I *share* words."

"How can you share words?" Tyler asked.

"You'll see," Daisy replied as the first parents came into the room.

Daisy's parents and Lily stopped to admire Emma's video and watch her perform. But Mrs. Bookman headed straight for Daisy's café, pulled out a chair and sat down.

Daisy handed her a menu.

Appetizers
Odes
Haiku
Free Verse

Main Courses
Word Lists

Desserts
Words for Sharing

"How delicious!" Mrs. Bookman said. "I'd like to start with an appetizer poem. How about a haiku?"

Daisy shared her favorite. "This one is called 'Green,' and I wrote it after my day at the creek with Emma," Daisy said, before reading the poem.

Green is all around
apple green, dark green, bright green.
Nature's best color?

Mrs. Bookman loved it! For her second appetizer, she selected free verse. Daisy explained how she had turned her list of *Cloud Words* into a poem.

"It's called 'Clouds,' " Daisy said.

Lying on my back,
I see them float by.
White and gray, fluffy and puffy,
full like cotton candy,
or thin and wispy.
Clouds.

"Daisy, it's just the way I remember!" Mrs. Bookman said. "Sitting and sharing words. How did you ever think of a Word Café?"

"I tried to come up with something *delightful* — something that would really make people smile," Daisy replied. "And I wanted it to be *different* from anything anyone else was doing."

"You succeeded!" Mrs. Bookman exclaimed.

Emma pirouetted up to Daisy's café table. She looked carefully at the menu. "I'd like to try an ode and a haiku, please," she said.

"Coming right up," Daisy replied. She read Emma the "Ode to Ice Cream."

"You're making me hungry," Emma said, reaching for one of Daisy's word cookies.

"You'll like this haiku," Daisy said. "It's about your favorite color." She read her haiku called "Pink."

Gray rocks line the creek.
Pink flowers surprise my eyes
poking through the cracks

Emma clapped her hands. More people wandered over, and Daisy shared more poems and some of her word lists. Soon words were flying, with people sharing their

favorites or remembering a word that made them think of a certain place or time.

"*Campfires*," said one dad.

"*S'mores*," called out another.

"*Sunflowers*," a mom offered.

"*Hush-a-bye*," said Mrs. Bookman, winking at Daisy.

"*Super duper!*" Samantha chimed in.

"*Teddy bears*," said Lily, who had come to stand next to Daisy.

Daisy beamed as words danced around her and cookies disappeared.

Chapter Ten

"I have something for you that's not on the menu," Daisy said to Miss Goldner, who had just come to the café. Daisy pulled a homemade card out of her bag. "I turned my list of *Room 8 Words* into a poem," she explained. "I used some words from the list and added a few new ones, too."

"Will you read it for me?" Miss Goldner asked.

Daisy was happy to.

A room seems like a simple thing,

just four walls and a door.

But I know that's not all it is,

because Room 8 is so much more.

It's inventing and learning together,

creating and sharing, too.

It's smiles and giggles and dancing,

and it's all because of you.

You use new words every day,

and always say, "Give it a try!"

You're the reason Room 8 is great,

and why it's hard to say good-bye.

"Thank you," Miss Goldner said, placing her hand over her heart to show how much the poem meant to her. "Good-byes are hard, but I will always remember Room 8."

"Me, too," Daisy said, handing the card to her teacher.

Miss Goldner saw that instead of signing her name, Daisy had drawn a daisy. She read the poem carefully. "It's beautiful," she said. "I can tell you worked hard on it."

She was about to continue, when one of the parents interrupted to ask her to say a few words. "Excuse me, Daisy," she said.

When she got to the front of the room, Miss Goldner clapped her hands to get everyone's attention. "Thank you so much for coming to our Student Showcase tonight," she said. "I know you will all agree with me that these students are very talented in so many different ways." All the parents, grandparents and visitors cheered.

"This is one of the last times we'll be together," Miss Goldner said. "I just want to thank my students for making it one of the best years ever for me as a teacher. I'll think of you often this summer, and when I'm at my new school, too. I especially want to thank you for making tonight so special. It really has been …"

She tried again.

"It's been just …" She faltered. "I'm at a loss for words."

All eyes in the room were on Miss Goldner.

Slowly, she turned to the back corner and reached out her hand.

"Daisy," she said, "I need a little help."

Daisy opened her notebook and quickly found what she was looking for. It was one of the words that described Room 8 perfectly

but didn't fit into her poem. Now she knew

just what to do with it. She came and stood

next to Miss Goldner, taking her teacher's

outstretched hand.

"It's been *spectacular*," Daisy said.

"Yes, that's exactly the right word!" Miss Goldner declared, wrapping Daisy in a huge hug.

"It's been a big night," Miss Goldner said. "Everyone looks so happy."

"I'm more than happy," Daisy said. She threw her arms up in the air as she exclaimed, "I'm absolutely spectacular!"

Daisy's Wonderful Word Lists

FAVORITE RHYMING WORDS

sweet — treat

flower — power

sun — fun

bright — light

look — book

ring — sing

yellow — mellow

MADE-UP WORDS

coolio — super

Iska-biska — How are you?

Ilpa-dilpa — Fine, thank you.

Mahatzi — Let's go!

glubby — feeling blah

kersapped — confused

poetrified — petrified about poetry

QUIET-TIME WORDS

good-night	sweet dreams
snuggle	dreamy
hush-a-bye	drowsy
lullaby	

PERFECTLY PAIRED WORDS

bouncy balls

chunky chocolate

comfy couches

flying flags

summer sun

CLOUD WORDS

cotton candy	wispy
white	fluffy
gray	puffy
floating	

POETRY WORDS

ode	rhyme
haiku	free verse

SWEETEST WORDS

chocolate!!!!!!	honey
taffy	fudge
caramel	ice cream
licorice	

NATURE WORDS

green   splish

gurgle   splash

rocks   wildflowers

trees

ROOM 8 WORDS

giggles   great

inventing   spectacular

sharing   creating

dancing   learning

awesome   smiles

Kids Can Press acknowledges the financial support of the Government of Ontario,
through the Ontario Media Development Corporation's Ontario Book Initiative;
the Ontario Arts Council; the Canada Council for the Arts; and the Government
of Canada, through the CBF, for our publishing activity.

Published in Canada by	Published in the U.S. by
Kids Can Press Ltd.	Kids Can Press Ltd.
25 Dockside Drive	2250 Military Road
Toronto, ON M5A 0B5	Tonawanda, NY 14150

www.kidscanpress.com

Edited by Debbie Rogosin
Designed by Julia Naimska
Series design by Marie Bartholomew

CM 14 0 9 8 7 6 5 4 3 2 1
Manufactured in Shenzhen, Guang Dong, P.R. China, in 10/2013
by Printplus Limited

Library and Archives Canada Cataloguing in Publication

Feder, Sandra V., 1963–, author
Daisy's big night / written by Sandra V. Feder ; illustrated by Susan Mitchell.

(Daisy)
ISBN 978-1-55453-908-6 (bound)

I. Mitchell, Susan, 1962–, illustrator II. Title. III. Title: Big night. IV. Series:
Feder, Sandra V., 1963–. Daisy.

PZ7.F334Dab 2014   j813'.6   C2013-904064-1

Kids Can Press is a *l'©rus*™ Entertainment company